The Motel

Copyright © Nick Voro 2024

First Edition

The Motel

VoroBooks, Etobicoke, Ontario, Canada

ISBN: 978-1-7383199-3-0

Typesetting and additional design by Lee Thompson Editing+

To contact the author: Nick_Voro@hotmail.com

THE MOTEL

YOU WOULD BE HARD-PRESSED to find a more remote place on any map. This passing thought raced through the busy mind of Timothy Price as he looked around the savage desert wasteland. He found the bareness of it all unsettling. Getting lost out here meant handfuls of sand before a drop of water would ever turn up—a slow, torturous death.

Timothy rested his elbows on the hot aluminum

handrail of the motel's second-story corridor. He shielded his eyes to see if he could spot anything else around, only to return to the single road by which he had arrived. Forking just once, Timothy had taken a left turn to reach this wonderful architectural landmark in the Nevada desert.

The motel stood dominantly over an inexhaustible expanse of sand. A raw deal, perhaps, but a motel superimposed in the middle of nowhere provided a great deal of anonymity to travelers whose lives depended on it.

Timothy hated that he was such a traveler. He had often landed in hot water, knew what being preyed upon was like. Except this was a few notches above the usual, involving an actual hideaway, with deadly consequences if he was caught. He was never the type to delude himself about his faults, never the type to not be able to name them if pressed on the spot about them. The only answers he fumbled were usually to the hard questions asked by toughs he encountered along the way. And those were always about money.

Borrowing money, how much was owed and repayment of that money. This partly explained how he ended up here, but did it matter in the end? The bottom line was he was here now, and he got here due to the addictive nature of his character and the fact that he owed much money to those very same toughs. And instead of the more sensible solution of actually paying back the money, Timothy decided to skip town.

He wiped his forehead with the back of his sleeve, irritated and utterly defeated—painstakingly trying to rouse his unresponsive mind.

Timothy consulted his watch—it was just after 6 PM. His hands plunged deep into the pockets of his dirty corduroys and fished out a pack of Camels. He dropped his head forward over his cupped hands, protecting the flame of a sparked match. As he raised his head, his peripheral vision intercepted something in the distance approaching at high velocity.

Sweat began to trickle down the back of his shirt. He stood stone still.

If it were daytime, he could attribute it to a mirage, but since it was evening all he could do was convince himself it was the product of a tired mind and the merciless heat. He tried in vain, tried his hardest to be a sceptic even when facing irrefutable truth, not daring to look away, continuing to fixedly stare at the swiftly approaching object. It was hard to make out any details at first, but as the object neared it caught the fading light, allowing Timothy to identify the emerging apparition as a classic '72 Corvette.

His quivering lips dislodged the cigarette firmly held in place just seconds ago. "*It's just a car,*" he kept repeating. It would not mean a thing to anyone but him...

He drew back, hyperventilating and trying to gulp at the stale evening air. His heartbeat reached a sickening crescendo while his shaky hands fumbled for the rusted doorknob of his room.

Once inside, he automatically pulled the tattered and faded curtain across the smudged window next to the door. He snapped the lock in place and connected the chain to the track, knowing full well it would not withstand the slightest pressure.

With his back against the door and his shoulders slumped, he felt helpless—an animal caged in a tiny room. The door did not even have a peephole. All he could do was stand there and listen for anything that would break the silence.

Minutes passed, nothing happened.

Timothy was not so easily dissuaded and kept on listening. Fear makes a person stubborn—especially when their life hangs in the balance. Finally, becoming decidedly impatient, he dropped to his knees and sprawled across the stained, foul-smelling carpet. He peered along the gap created by the door and held back a startled shout when he observed a pair of dark shoes on the other side.

Next to the stranger's shoes was Timothy's burning cigarette, which he had forgotten in his haste to hide inside his room. With disbelief, he watched as the red ember of the cigarette lifted from the floor and disappeared from his restricted vantage point. The cigarette never did reappear, nor had Timothy seen the hand that surely retrieved it from the ground. The man must be puffing on the cigarette, Timothy thought, and wearing black leather gloves that blended with the darkness of the evening.

He finally heard the man walk away, heard sounds in the room next door, and not long after Timothy's eyelids grew heavy, twitched, and drooped shut. He felt twice his age, worn out by sheer stress.

They have found me. No great surprise there. It was always just a matter of time.

Timothy awoke with his teeth clenched around the worn-out carpet. Dissatisfied with his polypropylene breakfast, he quickly spat it out. His back was stiff from sleeping on the floor. Then again, it was always stiff.

He stood up with all the briskness he could

muster and clumsily made his way to the bathroom sink where he vigorously scrubbed his face and rinsed out his mouth.

Slowly coming to, he recounted the final harrowing minutes of last night with increasing uneasiness. Fear once again doused him like the most pungent of colognes, fully rousing him. He began to pace the length of the room with great deliberation, obsessively darting his eyes between the front door and the cheap wall clock with its hope-crushing hands pronouncing nothing but continuing despair.

His life depended on a letter. Its contents would tell him if she were safe and if they could still rendezvous at the agreed location. He had to have it. However, for him to grab hold of it, he had to travel down to the manager's office on the first floor.

This, of course, meant leaving his room unoccupied with all his meager but valuable possessions.

Moreover, if his next-door neighbor happened

to be an assassin sent to kill him, he did not want to walk into a trap upon his return to the room.

An idea came to him. He put on his jacket and tore a loose thread from one of the sleeves. He licked the palm of his hand as well as the thread and left it there, glued to his palm, obscured from the sight of any prying eyes.

Timothy walked out into the sunshine and started to lock the door, covertly pressing the palm of his hand underneath the handle, positioning the thread there with one end sticking to the door and the other to the frame.

He descended the exterior stairs two at a time, clutching the rail for support and attentively listening for any noise.

Everything seemed calm.

The manager's office was the last door on the far left. He purposefully continued toward his goal, trying hard to ignore the distance, but something made him halt mid stride—the '72 Corvette. Parked directly in front of the manager's office, it had been blocked from the panoramic view of the second floor by the protruding awning.

His body tensed and his feet felt rooted to the walkway while his mind spun out of control with violent thoughts.

Was the stranger inside the office now?

Timothy knew that uncertainty feeds paranoia and fear. He also knew he had to dispel it. Summoning a fictitious surge of adrenaline, he yanked the door wide open and darted inside the office.

The office was a mess, littered with loose papers and junk stacked in pyramidal shapes, with no shortage of cobwebs and general filth that goes along with a place that has not seen a cleaning in at least a decade. There was also a sickening stench that lingered in the air and slowly crept up Timothy's nostrils. Covering his nose and mouth, he focused upon the wall-sized-unit behind the empty concierge's desk with its numerous identical boxes.

There was no letter in 10-B.

He had told her ahead of time where he would

be. He thought it would certainly reach here by now. That is, unless something went wrong...

"Can I be of service, monsieur?"

She startled him; he had overlooked her presence amidst the chaos. But there she was in her receptionist attire in the far corner, making her way toward the desk.

The surprise left Timothy temporarily mute. Noticing his lack of initiative, she addressed him cordially in slightly accented French, "I hope you found your room to your liking. It's fortunate that the gentleman who booked it in advance never checked in to claim it."

"You mean to tell me..."

"Yes, monsieur. It was the last room to get booked, if that's your question. We have a full booking at the motel."

"But I haven't seen anyone else around..."

"The customers like their privacy, monsieur. Naturally, we do everything in our power to meet their needs."

Naturally, thought Timothy. An array of

subversive lodgers staying at a motel with a reputation for tucking away murderers, gamblers, and other vagrants. Fate has a dark and twisted sense of humor. The only room that he was able to book had a last-minute cancellation. Cancellation by a much-wanted party, apparently, judging by the personage situated right next door.

This truly was the worst case of mistaken identity. It is not him that the man next door wanted. However, what could he do? He could not just knock on the door and explain all this to the potential murderer of the man who never showed up to claim his room. It was all a stretch, a jump to conclusions, but Timothy trusted his intuition, plus it simply added up. If they were business partners, had business to attend to, the stranger would have knocked on the door instead of threateningly standing outside the door without even considering knocking, wanting his presence kept a secret.

It was imperative at this point to return to the room and think it all over.

Timothy exchanged a weak goodbye with the woman and hurried back. Even with this new development he had a presentiment that something awful was going to happen before the day was up. A gambler always knows. As long as he could remember, Timothy had referred to it as, "Gambler's intuition." When the powers that be conspired against the player, delivering a storm of bad luck, too many terrible coincidences occurring not to know you are in the eye of a bad streak, and while it will eventually break or so goes the "Gambler's fallacy," it has to fulfill its purpose, and the player must decide whether to weather the storm or call it a day.

With this raging weather, these torrential thoughts, Timothy reached his room, so lost in his own mental downpour that he almost opened the door without checking for the piece of thread. He looked closely, but it was not there.

The stranger's timing was immaculate—able to lock pick his way inside the room and have a look around in a short amount of time.

Timothy opened the door with a trembling hand. He knew his face must be pale from unadulterated terror. He also knew he had to check the room. What if the stranger was still inside? Unable to get out in time. Now silently waiting. Hidden in the closet or underneath the bed. Biding his time. In his fear-stricken state, with his heart beating furiously and hands trembling uncontrollably, Timothy somehow mustered enough courage to check both hiding places, finding no other occupant except himself and the terrible tentacles of terror suffocating all life from him.

The room began to spin—his spellbound eyes traveling with the rotation until they finally settled on a picture of a yacht. It was the only picture in the room. One he had noticed earlier. A picture which was now slightly *askew*. Hung on the wall he shared with...

Timothy felt the weight and the futility of the situation. This was not good. Not good at all. A doomsday pronouncement was clearly upon him. He felt nervous, skittish, bathing in his own sweat unaided by this stiflingly hot room.

His mind brimmed with the worst possible thoughts; the type of thoughts that tend to disfigure perception and cloud over clear-headedness. He had gotten himself mixed up, entangled in a situation with absolutely no ability to call the shots.

Timothy had to do the unfathomable. He knew this, but he could not allow the idea to take its rightful place in his mind. He had to examine the back of the picture. To cross the room without raising suspicion: freedom of movement, something we take for granted every day. Timothy scanned the room. A desperate darting around his detention cell.

He stopped his search at his feet. His heavy leather shoes were utilitarian by all definitions, but were thick-soled, hindering him all the same. Sure, the room had wall-to-wall carpet, but the floor also had a squeak, he remembered. But where exactly? *God, what if he stepped on that godforsaken deficient noisy floorboard?*

Slowly, very slowly he started to bend his body forward with that knowledge never leaving his mind. Desperation emboldens people. It makes them fight and scratch for their dear life. They do not want to let go. Timothy was one of those. The not wanting to let go types. He wanted time, his time, as much time as he could get his hands on, fit in his grubby degenerate gambler's hands, and carry off with him. So, he went to the task at hand and began to untie his shoelaces.

Thankfully, the shoes untied rather easily, and he could slip his feet out after unfastening the laces a bit. His feet now free of their shackles, the day's perspiration able to roam the small quarters, a pungent aroma from his formerly incubated sweltering feet striking the inside of Timothy's defenseless nose, making him wince. But the shoes were off. This was not insignificant in any sense. A victory indeed, no matter how small. He smiled for the first time since he got here—a chance this all will not end in disaster.

Timothy set the shoes down next to the bed.

He fetched his travel bag resting on the one side and carefully undid the zipper. Inside the bag, he located a pair of tight leather gloves. He put these on to help with the slickness of his hands. The material quickly absorbed the moisture. He clasped his hands together, interlacing the fingers to help the absorption process along.

Now he had to climb the unassailable mountain—a figure of speech that never rang truer to Timothy than at this decisive moment. He straightened up, forfeiting his half-bent position over the bed.

Timothy took his first step forward. The wheels started to revolve; events set in motion. He could not stop now. There was no time to stand still and reflect on this one slight step forward. He had to follow it with more such steps and time was surely running out.

He resumed his tiptoeing, trying to tread lighter, dedicated to one, and only one task at hand, putting faith in each step, trusting that this forward movement would ameliorate the predicament he was in.

When he reached the picture, he knew this was the moment of absolute truth. The moment which would reveal to him whether he could genuinely face his demonic and thirsting fears and stand up to them, because to go back, there was not anywhere to go back to. To go back meant cellular death, the expiration of the flesh, a freshly dug-up grave reserved just for him to join the long list of dearly departed and soon forgotten individuals who once inhabited this earth.

He lifted the frame, thinking about his own placement in the world of the living things. On the back of this cheap, enlarged and framed photograph, a tiny jet-black device greeted him, the kind often described in dime-store spy thrillers, not that Timothy was ever a keen reader...

A listening device. A bug.

His worst-case scenario involving unlawful entry successfully fulfilled.

He had no doubts about what the stranger was doing at this very moment: conducting audio surveillance with this microscopic microphone, capturing and recording sound, dissecting and scrutinizing high spikes in volume.

Timothy thanked named and unnamed gods for the fact the picture frame had a string instead of a chain which would have scraped against the nail on which it hung, giving him away the moment he lifted the frame.

He knew he would have to remove the listening device. It was the only way. The listening device itself was power. It immured him to his smallish room, putting him at a great disadvantage, unable to leave without his captor knowing it.

Grasping the picture firmly with his gloved hands, he carefully moved toward the bed. This meant traversing the uneven terrain of the worn-out carpet—with areas exposing the squeaky rotting wood underneath. He feared the fateful creaking misstep, or worse, a toe-catching fall, the unmistakable thud.

Halfway across he realized he was not breathing. What if he passed out? He took a step. No creak. Then another. Silence. His lungs ached for air.

Six excruciating steps later, safely at the bed, lightheaded but able to breathe again, he placed the picture face down, the device dead center in the back of the picture like a hidden message, authorial inscription, a signature belonging to the sadistic surveillance expert on the other side of the wall. He knew he must hurry. With his right hand he reached out, trembling from the massiveness of the moment—everything surging inside of him. He tugged. The device did not budge. Fear seized hold of him. His face resembled a death mask. Sweat droplets fell from his forehead to the semi-carpeted floor.

He took a deep breath, trying his best to eradicate all negative thoughts, and reached for the device once more. This time he was able to carefully pry it away from the picture-backing, taking a moment to hold it between his gloved fingers in reverence—an aesthete admiring his priceless acquisition.

Now that Timothy had the object, he realized he never carefully thought-out all the details beforehand, such as what he would do with it once he had it in his hands. The story of his life: the doubting mentality of a self-defeatist. He would just have to wing it, improvise on the spot, an actor following instinct rather than script.

Through the process of disqualification, he settled for the bed, unblemished and unslept in as of the night before last. He placed the device in the middle and carefully smothered it with layers of bedding. Surely the only thing it would transmit now would be utter silence.

Now, with the device entombed in layers of cotton and polyester, Timothy, no longer worried about detection of his movements, returned the picture to its rightful place on the wall—*Bugger off you bug, he thought.*

As the string pulled taut, stretching itself to the limit against the rickety, corroded nail, he happened to recall his gambling past—hopefully, the past if he learns a lesson from this experience and lives to abide by a new way of living—where this current predicament mirrors precisely the moment in the game that propels most degenerate gamblers to continue to gamble. The moment when a lousy streak turns winning, turning the tables around on the croupier as a glimmer of hope shines through. Brief as it may be.

Timothy suddenly felt weak and collapsed on the bed, dehydrated, exhausted and starving. The room started to revolve. He felt as if he were in an oneiric state where everything he knew as being solid and dependable abruptly became a caricature of its former self. Nothing was durable, crumbling at a mere touch. There was a hollowness and collapsibility to everything, nothing had any soundness left to it, no longer check-marked and approved, classifiable as trustworthy, imperishability was a thing of the past. And so was he. Collapsing under pressure. Allowing darkness to reign.

*

Timothy stirred. His facial muscles twitched. He felt the overnight settled soreness that had spread throughout his body. His eyelids seemed stuck together. He fluttered them repeatedly until he was able to keep them open. Timothy knew he had fainted. He had suffered these fainting spells for a long time now due to his hereditary heightened stress reactions, and whenever he awoke for the inescapable return to the present, reality always seemed intrusive, especially after an episode of deliberate forgetfulness.

For the second time now, he found himself in a contorted position on the floor, splayed out awkwardly in the dark. He slowly raised himself up. A splitting headache besieged the cupola on top of his shoulders and neck. He felt terribly parched, and while the combination of the excruciating pain and the insatiable thirst were undoubtedly horrific, the incoming, invading thoughts were even worse. He shook his head from side to side, desperate to rid himself of them.

During this side-to-side headshake, indistinct

sounds from the great outdoors reached Timothy's ears. He stopped, stood, grabbed the closest wall to steady himself, and made his way over to the window. A bright light framed the door.

The involuntary tremble was back in his hands. With deliberate slowness, trying fruitlessly to escape the inevitable, he moved the curtain to one side, confronting a set of headlights. Someone else had arrived at the party.

He lost sight of the car once it travelled underneath the awning to park. Timothy had to rely on his ears now. First, he heard the declarative statement of a car door forcefully slammed shut. Then, the newcomer's quick footsteps leading up to the motel. A door opened and closed somewhere on the first floor. *Must be the manager's office*, thought Timothy. His heart began to pound—an erratic, quickening beat. His hopes of escape wilting.

The downstairs door *clanged* again, opened-and-shut by a robust hand unafraid of drawing attention to itself. A *jingling* sound followed. Had to be multiple keys on a key ring. Then, more footsteps, intensifying as the person neared. *I should run, I should do it now*, thought Timothy, but something held him back. He allowed the moment of hesitation to overrule all else and was now forced to endure the ever familiar feeling a person gets before their space is invaded. A moment of complete powerlessness.

Footfalls now sounded on the stairs. A confident, quickened pace. Timothy tried to swallow the lump in his throat, but there was not enough saliva for even that—an acidic taste permeated his entire mouth, making him nauseous the more he tasted it.

He looked around the room until his eyes returned to the front door. A whole other world awaited him beyond that locked door, if he could only open it. But he knew he would not even try. All he could do was stand and wait, consumed by every sound that reached him, by the nearby footfalls and all the other echoings in the night.

The footsteps finally came to a halt. There

was a change. All the other noises faded as if in preparation for the prophesied knock, which never did befall the brittle door. Just silence. Unnerving seemingly never-ending silence.

Timothy could not stay in the dark for long, and not learning his lesson the first time around, resorted to flattening himself on the floor once more, peering through the gap just in time to see what he could only describe as a sudden violent flash. Something described as a "golden splendor" in those chippie espionage paperbacks, his continual reference guide to all things above the low-level criminal activity he was used to. *A bullet. It had to be a bullet!* He could have sworn he even heard the muffled scream when the bullet pierced the soft tissue of the human body.

He did not have all the answers, he could only figure out certain parts, but the end result was clear enough. The matter of the murder itself was not a very complicated affair: it has taken place and produced a body (reasonable guess: the car-door-slamming newcomer) which was now being dragged away by the next-door neighbor.

The weapon, the originator of the "golden splendor," gave his neighbor god-like omnipotence. But even without the weapon, Timothy was no match for the man. He only had one course of action available now. To run as fast and as far as he could. Luckily, the disposal of the body allotted time for this final move, the betting of all the chips. All in, with everything to lose, including his life.

Timothy pivoted and directed his gaze toward the bathroom window. It transfixed him. Beyond the low-grade wooden frame still holding the smeared glass in place, was freedom. He could feel how tangible it truly was. Beyond that smudged window was a sand-swept terrain, a hidden Biblical desert, ready to welcome him, a foolish man, a captive saved by the immeasurable sand that resembles the sea.

Yes, this was the only definitive way. The front door was not. Not an option. Not even up for consideration. His mind raced forward, a tireless abacist calculating probabilities. *Would he fit?* It did not look advisable at all, especially for someone who feared heights.

Timothy approached the window, a hybrid of emotional states, hesitant yet hard-boiled. Looking for resolve, yet terrified of not finding it in the last available place. He tried the window; it did not budge. He tried it again. On the second attempt it yielded easily enough, and as he stared down from the highest point of the motel (excluding that of the rooftop) he could not help but wonder about the horrible, severe fall which awaited anyone unlucky enough to lose one's grip and balance. A toss-up between paralysis and a slow, agonizing death.

He was fully betting on himself to be the recipient of such a death, or paralysis. Either one was a distinctive possibility, if not a probability. *A fitting end to a subterranean life spent without a single crowning achievement,* Timothy thought, hardly a life worth envying. Some would even call this self-inflicted redemption, a mercy killing, a way to set things right.

Timothy knew he would try regardless, even if the odds had been entirely against him since his arrival here. Most people find it worthwhile to try to salvage something, up to a certain point, before throwing in the towel and checking out, resigning to their unchangeable fate and living out the rest of their lives with their heads down and hopes crushed. Few lucky ones succeed at beating the odds, winning the fight against that unwavering belief of some in the predetermined destiny of their lives and gain the ability to manufacture their own life anew.

He turned away from the window. Prolonged staring would not change the possible outcomes of his self-proposed great escape. He shook his head and walked back into the room. Everything would have to happen with exactitude and precision. One does not just scale down the side of a motel without preparation beforehand.

Not to mention that thirty feet of rope was not included with the fresh linens and toilet articles. He would have to improvise, most likely settle for the bedsheets, making sure to twist them all the way around until they resembled a cable of cotton strong enough to hold his weight. Once he touched solid ground, he would have to make his way to his car completely unobserved. Making it not only a great, but a brazen escape, to say the least.

The preparations took time. A half hour vanished. Forfeited time, irreclaimable minutes and seconds Timothy would not be getting back, but miraculously the perfect amount for him to construct his makeshift rope. He knew he had pushed his luck. That the Reckoning Hour was now upon him. His self-indulgence for survival had landed him on the ledge of the motel's second-story window, his hands gripping the twisted bedsheets. He looked down at concrete and sand. The height was the barrier. *Surely the knots would fail.* One could call this an individual's protestation in the face of a calamitous set of circumstances, ones surely to result in death. Although, he might live to tell the tale.

A wave of numbness suddenly seeped through him. Timothy's mind was now at a standstill. No profundity of original ideas, not the flimsiest impression of a thought. *How could this be?* He looked back at the room, the door. Then he looked back down again. It should have been an uneventful stay. It did not work out according to plan. *Nothing ever does anyway.*

He took a step forward. His foot never connected with a solid surface, and Timothy plunged ahead. His free fall lasted only seconds before his makeshift rope did its part, propelling him back toward the side of the building, making him collide violently with the edifice. His left shoulder bore the brunt of the impact, which stiffened up his entire body.

Timothy did not dare let go, knowing full well his hard landing would create too much disturbance. He persisted, carrying on, enduring incredible pain with his hands clutching desperately to the rope, descending slowly toward solid ground.

And then it happened, just as it had happened before—everything became nebulous. And he knew that his hands would let go. Knew all too well that he would plummet below, unconscious by this point, finally impacting with the ground; the culprit responsible for putting a stop to his fall.

"Where am I? What is this? It's you... Look... It's all been a big misunderstanding. I know I am not the one you want. What could you possibly want with me? I am no one. No one of any importance. No one to catch the attention of someone of your stature. It's all been a piece of bad luck. A terrible coincidence. I've never even seen your face. I can't even see it now with the sun positioned behind you. I don't even know your name. Or the reason you are here. I know absolutely nothing about your business

here. I was just frightened. That's why I ran. I am easily spooked. I heard a noise that made my blood run cold. I thought someone was lock-picking my door, trying to rob me in the middle of the night. That's all it was. I swear. I never saw a thing. I just heard something that frightened me. You have to believe me. Please put that shovel down. I beg you. You don't need to do this. I am an innocent bystander. There is no need for this. You have no reason to eliminate me. To bury me out here in the middle of the desert. I saw nothing. I am telling you, I just got spooked. A loud noise startled me, that's all. Just rotten luck. That's all this is. Who am I? I am no one. A degenerate gambler evading loan sharks holed up in a run-down motel in the middle of the desert. You see, absolutely no one to worry about. I am so tiny in the grand scheme of things. A man who spent his whole life evading. Evading responsibilities and creditors. Always on the run from someone I owed money to. But I know you aren't one of them. I know it's not a case of that. I am just a parasite. A degenerate on the move.

Been running my whole life. Had an early start in childhood before the other kids and never stopped. You have no idea how exhausting it is. To never be able to catch your breath. Constantly looking over your shoulder. Please put that shovel down. It's all just one big mistake. I am not the one you want. How can I be? I am no one. A great big nothing. A roach under the floorboards of this motel. Aren't you tired of shovelling? Put the shovel down for a moment. Take a break. You are right, my teeth are chattering. And yes, I am talking excessively. I can't help it. I am anxious about being buried alive in the middle of this godforsaken desert. Forgive me. But no, I don't think anything can alleviate this stress unless you stop filling this hole. What's this you've thrown. I didn't mean to imply at me. I am sorry I can't seem to find the right words. A book? But how can this help? Read the title? You want me to read the title. A Spy's Espionage Story... this can't be. It can't be the same book. That's the book I kept thinking about the whole time. Trying to remember the name. I don't understand. How can you possibly have this book? A thrift store on the way to the airport? A dollar? What do you mean, it makes sense? Nothing makes sense about this. Fate? This can't be fated. How could I have ever considered the possibility this was meant to happen? I am not clairvoyant. I am not a fortune teller. Stop. Please stop shovelling! No. I can't just stop talking. If I stop I... That's easy for you to say. Resign sure. Just resign to my fate. It's inescapable. I have no control over what is happening to me. That's easy for you to say! How can this be... this can't be right? An infinitude of possibilities all converging to the same outcome. You are insane. A madman! Each and every time... The exact same outcome? You believe in this? I am not the person you want. Don't you get it?! I am an innocent bystander. Our paths weren't always going to cross. That's just not true. Insanity... what insanity. What roles... what script to follow? I have no idea what you are talking about. Prefigured by someone else for us? By whom?! God? You are saying you are the killer; other man was the intended target, and I was the innocent bystander? I have no idea what you are talking about. Killed whom? I hadn't even seen anyone else here except the woman tending the front desk. Stop shoveling. Just stop, will you? For godsakes stop! And stop telling me to resign to my fate. It doesn't add up, don't you see? It's erroneous. An erasure of everything that has led up to this moment. No, I don't think it fits. Stop. Just stop! This can't be real. I must have fallen and died. That's it, I just never made it down that makeshift rope. I let go, which isn't surprising with my weak upper body strength. I let go, and I fell down. Either killed on impact or sprawled on the concrete unconscious, bleeding out from a head wound. This can't be real. This cannot be my reality. This is something else. I fell asleep. Maybe I never even left the last casino, fallen over the slot machine, drunk, still clutching the handle. What do you mean prepare? Prepare for what? The death of hope? Please don't. The sand is already up to my neck. Please have mercy on me. Spare me. Please... I am begging you!"

ABOUT THE AUTHOR

A native of Kyiv, Ukraine, but living in Canada since the age of eleven, Nick Voro discovered literature at an early age, never quite mustering the ability to put an excellent book down. A recent graduate of the Toronto Film School, Nick divides his time between being a full-time parent and a full-time author.

His debut work, *Conversational Therapy: Stories and Plays*, has recently sold over 200 copies and is part of the library system (United States, Canada, New Zealand, Australia and Scotland).

Lee D. Thompson, an editor and writer from Moncton, New Brunswick, Canada, edited this short story. His books include: a novel in [xxx] dreams from Broken Jaw Press, Mouth Human Must Die from Frog Hollow Press and Apastoral: A Mistopia from Corona/Samizdat. His short fiction has been published in many anthologies, including Random House's Victory Meat, New Fiction from Atlantic Canada and Vagrant Press's The Vagrant Revue of New Fiction. He is the winner of the David Adams Richards Prize (2018) and New Brunswick Book Award (2022). He is the publisher of Galleon Books.